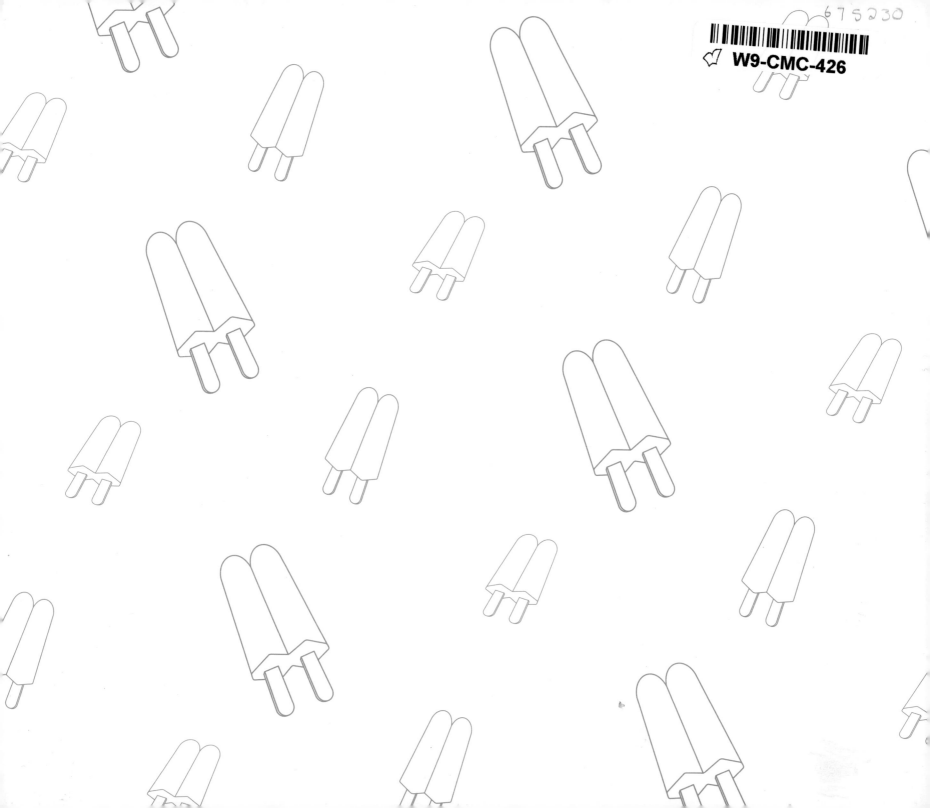

*To the ladies of Almey Court -
Denise, Kim, Lou, Nancy, Terry
and in memory of Donna.* – *Jane Barclay*

To my mother. – *Janice Donato*

Barclay, Jane, 1957-
How Hot Was It?
Text © 2003 Jane Barclay
Illustrations © 2003 Janice Donato

Published by Lobster Press™
1620 Sherbrooke Street West, Suites C & D
Montréal, Québec   H3H 1C9
Tel. (514) 904-1100 • Fax (514) 904-1101 • www.lobsterpress.com

Publisher: Alison Fripp
Editor: Kathryn Cole
Graphic Design & Production: Tammy Desnoyers

Distributed in the United States by:
Publishers Group West
1700 Fourth Street
Berkeley, CA 94710

Distributed in Canada by:
Raincoast Books
9050 Shaughnessey Street
Vancouver, BC V6P 6E5

We acknowledge the financial support of the Government of Canada through the Book Publishing Industry
Development Program (BPIDP) for our publishing activities.

The Canada Council | Le Conseil des Arts
for the Arts | du Canada

We acknowledge the support of the Canada
Council for the Arts for our publishing program.

National Library of Canada Cataloguing in Publication

Barclay, Jane, 1957-
       How hot was it? / Jane Barclay, author ; Janice Donato, illustrator ; Kathryn Cole, editor.

ISBN 1-894222-70-9

       I. Donato, Janice II. Cole, Kathryn III. Title.

PS8553.A74327H693 2003   jC813'.54   C2002-905727-2
PZ7

Printed and bound in China.

HOW HOT WAS IT?

Written by
Jane Barclay

Illustrated by
Janice Donato

Lobster Press™

It was a **muggy,**
   sluggy,
   hair-teasing,
       air-squeezing,
can't-get-out-of-bed,
both-legs-filled-with-lead
            kind of hot.

Outside my window I heard the electric buzzzzz
of cicadas from high up in the trees.

I lay in bed and watched dust flecks
floating up a sunbeam. I waited for
the whisper of a breeze.

In the kitchen a fan whirred back and forth, stirring up the soupy air.
My dog nudged my knee with his nose.
"Bow-w-out, bow-w-out," he begged.
"It's too hot to go out, Dog," I said.

How hot was it?

It was a **grueling,**
drooling,
tongue-dragging,
tail-sagging
nose-pressed-to-the-door,
flop-down-on-the-floor
kind of hot.

I sat at the table and peeled myself an orange. In the yard a shiny black bird flapped its wings and shook dirt through its feathers. Across the fence, our neighbor's laundry hung limp and heavy on the clothesline.

I could hear my dad
getting ready for work.
He came into the kitchen wiping
his face with a handkerchief.
"Whew! It's hot out there," he said.

How hot was it?

It was an **icky, sticky,**
nerve-grating,
tie-hating,
wish-I'd-fixed-the-air,
grouchy-as-a-bear
kind of hot.

It was time to go to school. I put on my sandals and my sun hat, and my mom covered me with lotion. I slipped out the door and trudged down the sidewalk, my sandals slapping the cement. I passed hoses that lay coiled on the grass like snakes sleeping in the sun, and sprinklers that hissed and spit on scorched lawns.

In the schoolyard, the sun baked the slide and the swings sat empty as we stood wilting in the heat. Inside, we slumped at our desks and the teacher said, "My, it's hot out there."

How hot was it?

It was a **sizzling,**
fizzling,
record-breaking,
belly-aching,
faces-red-as-beets,
shorts-stuck-to-our-seats
kind of hot.

In art class I painted my piñata.
In storytime the teacher read a
book about the equator, and in
math I shared a popsicle and
learned all about fractions.

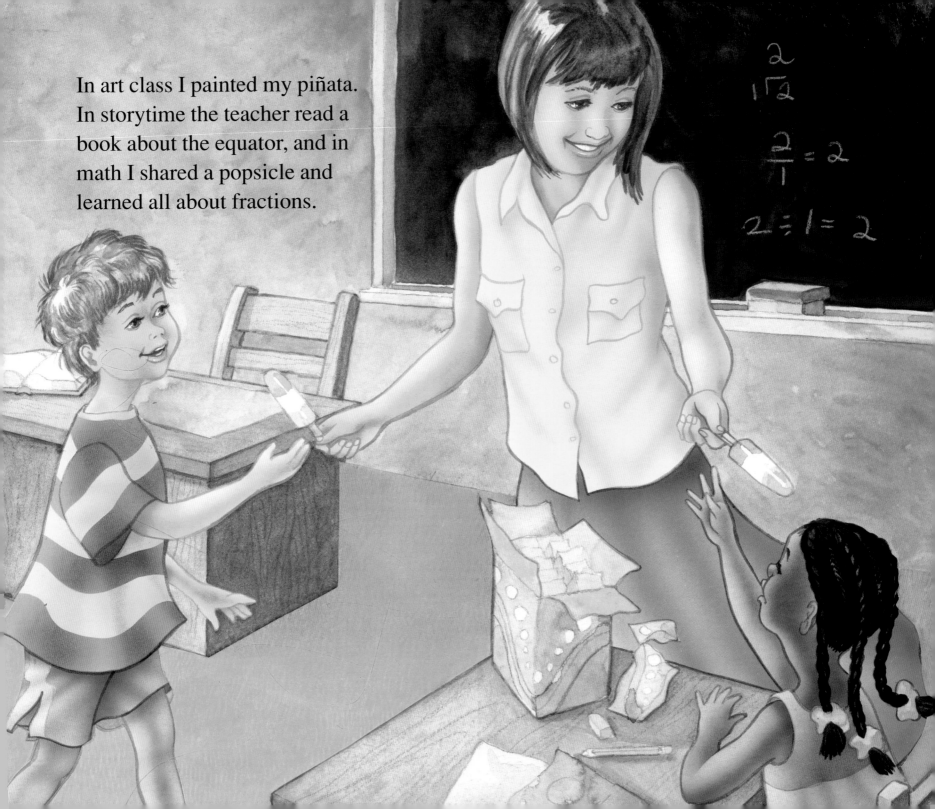

When the last bell rang, I braced myself for the walk home. I pulled my sun hat down to my eyes and opened the door. The heat pounced on me and licked at my popsicle. I hurried past the playground, the juice running down my arm. I paused at the sewer grate. Heat rose from the pavement in shimmering waves and I wondered if a dragon slithered underneath. I dropped my popsicle down the grate.
"Helloooo, down there!" I called and thought I heard a rustle in the musty darkness.
When I finally made it home, my mom said,
"Goodness! You look hot."

How hot was it?

It was a **roasting**,
toasting,
boiled-hamming,
toe-jamming,
fry-an-egg-or-two,
chillies-in-a-stew
kind of hot.

After my snack, Mom asked me to bring some chives from the backyard. Sweat trickled down my face as I crouched in the garden. A mosquito whined in my ear as I snipped, my shirt clinging to my back.

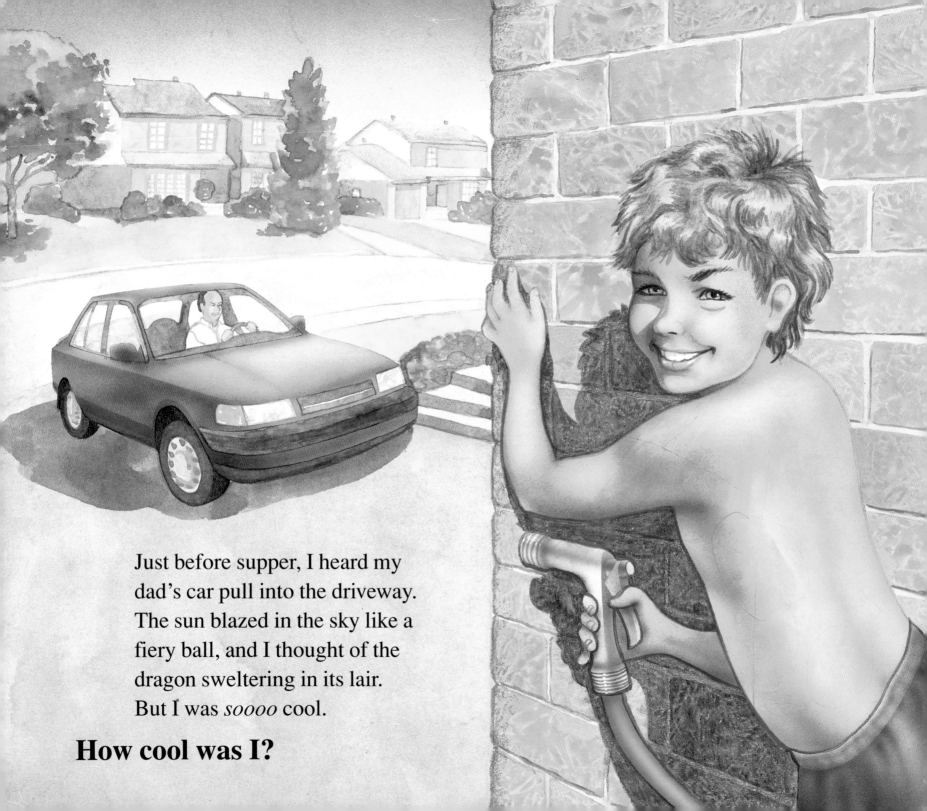

Just before supper, I heard my dad's car pull into the driveway. The sun blazed in the sky like a fiery ball, and I thought of the dragon sweltering in its lair. But I was *soooo* cool.

How cool was I?

It was a **pool-filling,**
pail-spilling,
thirst-quenching,
Dad-drenching,
ice-cold-lemonade,
hammock-in-the-shade
kind of cool.